Copyright 2019 by Ronald Vaden
All rights reserved
Printed in the United States of America

30786550R00036

Published by Amazon, Kindle Publishing

Story Written
by
Ronald Vaden

Special Thanks to:
Daughter Tameika Gleason
&
Stephanie Hill
For Giving me the stone that triggered the thoughts, and thanks to Belinda Dobbins for the encouragement to Write this short Story

"Thank God for the Gift of Writing"

*I'm Dedicating this Book to all my friends
And a Very Special Dedications to
My Family
To My Mother
Corredur M. Vaden
To My Brother
Jackie R. Vaden*

*And to All My Children
Ronnell F. Vaden
Tameika E. Gleason
Evan C. Vaden
Corredur J. Vaden
Maryal L. Vaden
Jacquelyn D. Vaden
And always In Memory of Brother
Rickie D. Vaden*

Table of Contents

Chapter 1
Just Star Gazing

Chapter 2
The First Discovery
"The Travel"

Chapter 3
The Second Discovery
"The **Switch**"

Chapter 4
The Third Discovery
"Changing Places"
The Elementary School Visit

Chapter 5
The Fourth Discovery
"Don't Touch the Stone!"

Chapter 6
You've been served

Chapter 7
"I lied and I'm sorry

Chapter 8
The Fifth Discovery
The Plantation

Chapter 9
A Reversal Was Made

Chapter 10
The Stone Necklace
"No Power"

Chapter 11
The Sixth Discovery
"The Voice"

Chapter 12
Just a Rock and
Somebody told me

Acknowledgments

I love to write, and I have a very vivid imagination and I find this is a good way of expressing my thought in this book. The idea came to me first when I was given a Good Luck Stone as a gift, and then came my having dreaming of the stone, and the thoughts started to overwhelm me with ideas of a story that could be told about the stone. I was spiritually inspired to write this book, and each night there was more being added to the story. There was a message that was given to me to be passed on to you the reader. I hope that you too will see the message that this short story holds. To be in someone else's shoes just for a moment that is suffering, what a difference it would make in how we see ourselves. The Reversal will try and paint that picture in very simple to understand stories as you travel with me back in time to make a difference. If you only had the power, could you, and Would you try and make a difference?

I want to thank you for taking the time to read this story, I do hope you will enjoy the trip into the past for just a little while and see how wonderful life could have been if a few people could have had a Reversal of the Mind and Heart.

I am very grateful to have written this story about the what ifs. I truly thank God for the gift of writing. I thank all of you in advance for your support and encouragements. I love all of you!

Ronald Vaden

The Reversal

Chapter 1
Just Star Gazing

The time was June 26, in the year 2000, it was a warm clear night for gazing into the galaxy to watch the splendor of this vast universe. I was so anxious to try out my new Extra powerful Telescope that was designed to reach deep into the dark galaxy world of space. I had my scope all set up to watch the night skies. I thought to myself "The conditions are perfect tonight for star gazing."
Boy! "This Telescope is powerful!", the moon looks close enough to reach out and touch. The planets were within sight, the Rings of Saturn I've never seen it this clear and distinct before. I wanted to shoot as far as possible with this new unit. I stretched this powerful baby to it's limits.

I panned the scope as far as I could into the outer most reaches of space. I was trying to see that far distant Andromeda Nebular if only my scope would just pull it off, that would really make my night!

Wait! I spotted an unusual object that was moving fast across the sky with a strange glow that was lighting up the dark deep space. I wondered was it a meteor or was it maybe just a falling star? I had not seen this type of behavior before. There was some erratic movement with this object it seems to have changed directions, and I notice it was headed directly towards earth or so it seemed and moving very fast.

Now this object is starting to get all my attention and I continued to watch the movement of this foreign object as it continued its onward approach towards our earth.

I was sure it was even closer than when I first noticed it. This object was getting bigger and brighter as it rapidly moved thru the sky. I was becoming very concerned about this issue, I wanted to seek some assistance, but it was happening so fast that I was not able to react. This object is on a direct course towards me as if it had a lock on my location. I began to panic and started gathering my equipment and taking it all down, and running back to my truck for cover as quickly as I could, but my time had expired, and it was upon me before I knew it, and as I reached to open the door the Light was so intense the shock wave of its impact caused a strange wave that went thru me I became dizzy, it burned with such intensity and I was knocked into my truck unconscious, and I was out for some time.

I'm not sure how long I was unconscious, but it seemed to have been quite a while. When I tried to start my truck the battery was completely dead, the truck was covered in dirt as if it had been here for some time now, and even the scenery has somehow changed and the weather was different, because I do remember that it was a June midsummer night when I was sky watching, and now the temperature is very cold and the trees are bare and the grass is all brown! What has happened here and where am I? I started walking back towards the main road to find some help. I was able to wave down a passing car. It was a young teenage driver that stopped and gave me a ride back to my truck and gave me a jump start. After thanking the driver for stopping and giving me some assistance, I was quick to ask what day was this? He responded, "why it's the 26th of December" and slowly I ask "and what year? "why it's 1999!" I was so amazed to find out that it was six months earlier and the month was not June it was December a year earlier, I question again, and the driver was perplexed that I would be asking the same question again, but this just could not be! It just could not be! I had been sent back in time! *I* was not completely clear what had taken place, I was still trying to piece this all together. I was now back at home, and still not clear what all had happened to me, but it was obvious that something had happened my decorations were still up, just getting over Christmas, Wow! I could not explain to anyone what had taken place with me, but something was different I could feel it. I've been completely moved back in another time zone, and nothing is making any sense to me, what happened to me out there that night? *"Go back to the site"*, Hmm? did I just hear someone's voice? Or am I just thinking out loud to myself? Maybe I needed to go back to the Site where this has happened to me and maybe I could piece this thing together. I needed some answers.

Chapter 2
The First Discovery
The Travel

U̲pon returning to the locations after several days had passed. I began walking around the area trying to find something that could give me some answers, and I found the impact area of whatever had hit the earth. It had been buried within the ground, and I began to dig into the soil. The hole was large at the opening, but got smaller the deeper I dug, and I finally found this round object that seems to have broken open, and a gel-like substance was all around it, and inside I saw this glowing small object I reached down with my shovel and fished it out of it's containment. It was small enough to fit in the palm of my hand.

It was a small Stone smooth and pearl-like, yet it sparkled like a fine diamond, the colors were strange and radiant I couldn't begin to describe.

I'd never seen anything like this before. I held the Stone and was admiring its beauty when I notice that while rubbing it with my fingers the Stone started to become warm and the more I rubbed the warmer it became. I began to have those same feelings as when I was first exposed to that bright light from the sky, I could feel myself getting dizzy, and the day was winding backward I could see the evening going back toward morning. I quickly drop the Stone and immediately time Stopped. Wow! What just happened? There's something very strange about this Stone. There're some special powers that this Stone has. I picked the Stone up and place it in a metal container and hurried back home. My curiosity had reached its's peek, and boy was I puzzled about this Stone. I continue to try and understand the power that it had, and how to control it if possible.

"why not try holding the Stone in your left and right hand," again am I hearing things?! I tried holding the Stone in both my right and my left hand, and I discovered that if it was in my right hand, I could move forward in time to present day, and if it was in my left hand I could move back in time. The longer I rubbed the Stone the further I went either into the future or into the past, but I notice that when going into the future I could only come back to present day, and I notice that the time upon my return to the present day the time would not have changed by many minutes even though I know I was gone for hours not just a few minutes. I could not go into the future, but I could go back in time for years and years! Now that I knew this I was able to return to the present time zone from where this had all started from which is now Friday, June 30, 2000. Things were so different with me now, I could not fully understand the true meaning of all of this, but I knew now that I had acquired a special gift that even I

could not explain. What else is in this power that this Stone possess?

During the weeks that follow I kept the Stone in my possession all the time, usually in my pocket, and It continued to amaze me with the powers that it holds.

Chapter 3
The Second Discovery
The Switch

Each day I've been going back in time by just a day and then a week and sometimes a month just to see what the effects would be on me, but each time the travel was smooth and rewarding, because I could remember so many things that I'd already done, I was having Déjà vu moments. Funny I could tell a person what they were going to say before they said it, and "how did you know that I was going to say that?", they would always ask. "but that was my little secret."

One night while I was out and not doing any Reversal of travel I discovered something even more unique about the Stone. There was yet another stage of power that I knew nothing about. I seem to have my hand in my right pants pocket where the Stone was located

So I would always be in the present time stage. I was out one late night and was pumping gas at one of those self serve all night gas stations, which I had to get some gas. I usually would wait till I was on my last gallon before I'd stop for gas. While pumping my gas someone came up and was trying to rob me. I was not sure what to do it happened so fast, and he had me at gunpoint he demanded my wallet. I begged for him not to shoot me, my mind was racing fast. I reached in my pocket for my wallet which was usually in my front pocket and felt the Stone, but the wallet was in my left pocket, I kept my hand in my right pocket with my hand on the Stone I could feel it getting warm. I knew it would not take me into the future, but I wanted to escape from this robber. I reached into my left pocket where the wallet was, but I never took my hand out of my right pocket where the Stone was, I could feel it was getting warmer and warmer till it was almost impossible to hold onto it! I reached to hand the wallet to the robber and his hand touched my hand, and instantly I was the robber with the gun now on him! and he was the victim! Wow! I thought to myself "I am robbing him and he's now pleading with me!", he falls to his knees and begs me not to shoot him! "What just happen here," he screamed at me, "what's going on here!" Now I knew what had happened it was the power of the Stone, there had been a **Switch**. I was now him and he was now me! I played the role for a moment just to give him total fear, and when I knew he had reached the point of total fear I touched him and the **Switch** was back being ourselves, but there was no gun, I had made sure of that. He was a changed man upon the **Switch** back he ran away in total fear and amazement, and so was I at what I had in my possession was a Stone of great power. I guess Being a robber is no longer anything he's interested in doing anymore. Oh! Boy Look out World, here comes the Power of the Stone!

Chapter 4
The Third Discovery
Changing Places
The Elementary School Visit

I had gotten to where I was becoming more in tune with the Stone and how touching it in certain ways would cause different results. I seem to be able to hear voice commands of dates, and suggested thoughts of places, and I could somehow be there just by changing the locations of the Stone around my presence, now I've learned that by moving it from the front pockets to the back pockets left and right

Side I could change my position as being an onlooker in time, and no one would Know that I was even present. Oh! And I also have the power to **Switch** the people that I am observing without having to even touch them, just hold the Stone for full intense heat and speak the word "**Switch**". One night while lying in bed and my mind racing at 90 to nothing I began to wonder about my elementary days, not that I needed to re-live them just some thoughtful memories of those early years. My mental thoughts were on September 7, 1965 just seem to stick out as a day I needed to make just one statement, Just one. An old friend needed some help I had heard about this long before now, so why not look in on that situation. Names are not necessary right now just the facts. He was just entering into the sixth grade and was in one of the toughest teacher's classes of her time, (so the students thought). They were in a reading session and each were all given an opportunity to read a paragraph from this book.

While this young girl was reading, which (I could tell was from a well to do family) did not pronounce a word correctly and the teacher instantly told her the correct pronunciation and she read on. Then it was this boy's turn to read the next paragraph, (and he was from a not so wealthy family) the teacher was at her desk listening to the readers and while reading he came upon a word that he'd never seen before, and he stumbles to pronounce the word, but was failing badly. The teacher continues to ask him to pronounce the word, and he replied I've never seen this before, and she said to pronounce the word! And again, he tried but failed again. Now the teacher is up from her desk with anger in her voice, and standing over him screaming "pronounce the word!", but every time he tried he failed, she would not tell him how to pronounce the word instead she would give in one hard slap on his back with this very large leather belt with force, and shouting No!, pronounce the word!. You could hear the sound of her voice and the slapping of the leather belt echoing down the hallway. This was being repeated over and over again, and each time he failed to get it right she would give him a hard lick across the back. I thought to myself "why don't you tell him how to pronounce the word instead of trying to beat it out of him?" I was getting upset with this action and knew I needed to do something to this unfair act. I reach my hand into my back pocket where the Stone was located and I held on to it till it had reached the full intensity and I Spoke the word, "**Switch**!!", and in an instant the teacher that was doing all the beating and screaming was now the student, I could tell from the expressions on her face that something had gone seriously wrong, but there was nothing she could do about her new found situation. She tried to pronounce the word that was so hard for the student, and now she can see that he's never seen this word before. She herself could now see that she (the student) could not pronounce the word!, and each time she got it wrong the belt came down on her back with a loud shout of No! Try again! She was having a very difficult time trying to figure out what has happened to her, she's now in his shoes and not doing very well. I once again held the Stone and allowed it to reach full intensity again and I spoke again "**Switch**", and she was again back at being a teacher, and just as she was getting ready to strike the student again she brought the belt down and looked at the belt, she drops the belt to the floor, and slowly return to her seat with total puzzlement on her face. The classroom was completely silent and surprised. The boy looked up at the teacher with tears in his eyes and repeated these words, "I don't know how to pronounce this word," and the teacher replied, "yes I know, it is a very difficult word to pronounce, and yes you are so right you've never seen that word before". She broke the word down and told him how to pronounce all the syllables by telling him how to pronounce the word. Quietly she the teacher sat at her desk and cried at the action that she had displayed that day. Sometime later after visiting that class in later years, the teacher seems to have a different demeanor as to how she taught her students mostly due to her finding fairness and less favor, and more patience to all the students in her classroom, She had removed her Taskmaster attitude altogether, I guess she wasn't too in favor of being beaten herself for reasons of very little value. Wearing someone else's shoes has somehow given her a different way of seeing things.

Chapter 5
Fourth Discovery
Don't touch the Stone!

The thought had crossed my mind about taking it on the road and seeing what the travel was like in the early nineteen hundred's. I had often heard how difficult it was to travel by car if you were a black person across some parts of the southern states, and especially at night so I had heard. So why not take the trip back to that great southern state of Mississippi. I held the Stone in my left hand and rubbed and I began to think of Thursday, May 3, 1945, the town is Sardis, the time is around 10 P.M. at night, and I was alone and driving in a very nice expensive Cadillac, nice and red with lots of chrome. I chose to go right through the heart of the city down highway 315 driving the speed limit. The night was quiet not much traffic around these parts, I guess it must be true what they say, "better be off the road by sundown boy!".

It wasn't long before I spotted the black and white backed in between two buildings, and yes, I wanted him to see me driving through his town at night. Sure enough, he spotted me and here comes the law. He didn't put his lights on immediately he followed me all the way out of town before the lights came on, and so I politely pulled over and waited for the officer to approach me, this may not be a good idea to just set here, but I'll take my chances. Slowly he walked up to the back of the car with his big flashlight beaming through my back window as he examined my car I didn't dare make a move.

Finally, he was standing at my driver's side window, I rolled down the window and before I could say anything he spoke with a very country southern voice, "what are you doing in this fine car nigga?" I replied, "it belongs to me officer," "you're lying Boy!" said the officer. Don't you know you're not allowed to drive thru my town at night boy? I replied "I guess I didn't see the sign Officer," the officer angerly snapped "there ain't no sign! You got a Smart mouth!, Get out the car Boy.

I tried showing my registration and driver's licenses, but that was not even necessary he had one thing on his mind and that was to harass me as much as he could. I stepped out of the car and I needed to get my hands on the Stone that was in my right pocket just in case I needed to immediately move back to the present day before something bad happened to me, but I dare not come out with my hand in my Pocket that would really change this tempo so I came out of the car with hands out. The officer motioned me to go to the back of the car where all the headlights were on me. He had me to empty my pockets and I thought this was my opportunity to get my hand on the Stone! As I reached into my pockets to empty them and grab the Stone the officer grabbed and pulled my arm, and when he did the Stone fell out on the ground and of course, the officer saw it. He reached down and picked up the Stone and said "well, well, what do we have here? As he admired it, he was mesmerized by the Stone, "looks like I've got myself a diamond doesn't it boy?" I replied, "officer its not a diamond it's just a rock that I carry around for Good Luck", "well boy, looks like your luck just ran out". Officer I asked, "could you please give it back to me it's of no value", and his reply was "boy I know a diamond when I see one and if it's not, it's still a very expensive Stone, and I think I'd better hold on to it". I was watching his fingers start to gently rub the Stone, "officer please don't rub the Stone, please don't! "what's the matter Boy! You afraid a genie is going to pop out", and he laughs Oh did he laugh! I did not know what would happen myself, but I knew something was going to happen, I just didn't want him to be sent back in time and leave me here in this red neck black hating Town. Before I could beg again "Please officer, don't rub…. suddenly his fist closed tightly on the Stone and he was frozen motionless and he began to scream loudly "my hand is burning!, My hand is burning! get this damn thing out of my hand!" I too stood speechless not knowing what to do. He started foaming at the mouth and still screaming, and fell to his knees, and as he was bowing down to the ground his fist opened up and the Stone fell to the ground, and immediately I picked up the Stone and put it in my pocket. I didn't leave the officer I just stood there for a moment, and finally, he staggered to his feet, and stared at me with fear in his eyes, "what just happened to me?" I didn't answer instead I simply said officer may I go now? And quickly he says very confusingly yes you can go, Mister. Mister? I thought to myself, Wow! What just happened here? Went from Boy to Mister all in one Night! As I was leaving I turned and said, "Oh by the way Officer Sir, there are more just like me that will be coming through your town and all of them carries that type of Stone. So it may be a good idea if I were you to allow them safe passage, and whatever you do, don't touch them or the Stone, Good Nite, Officer". As I was about the return to my car the officer spoke: "the unfair treatment and unnecessary harassment of Negro people is something I no longer have any desire to ever do again". I drove away with the officer still standing, staring and totally confused as to what just took place that night in Sardis Mississippi. Now I've Discovered another power that the Stone has, and it's very personal, **"Don't touch the Stone!"**

Chapter 6
You've been served

It was suggested that I see more of the south with the aid of the stone, it was something I guess I needed to see. I focus my mind on April 13, 1956, and travel back in time to a place of Memphis, Tennessee. Once again, I am driving late evening and I have to find a hotel for the night. Well, not having a GPS for directions this may not be so simple, but I find on my car seat a book that I am not familiar with it's called the Green Book, and there is a list of Hotels and Places to Eat for Blacks just traveling Through, this may just be what I need, Thanks. I found a Hotel that looks good for an overnight stay, it was the Hotel Clarke, located in downtown Memphis at 144 Beale Street. There are only 12 rooms, and it's on the second floor. I notice a sign over the front that read ""The Best Service for COLORED ONLY". Wow! looks like I am in the heart of Memphis' African-American business district.

I think maybe the stone and I will be safe here for the night. The Night is full of music and very active. Well, the night was uneventful, I slept well. I checked out of the hotel with a whopping $4.00 bill to pay with a big smile on my face. I was now out to find some food. I decided to drive away from the district that I was in, and travel to the not so favorable side of town, which was the main downtown of Memphis. I decided to park the car, while walking, looking and observing the

signs that were posted that read: "We cater to whites only, No Colored's allowed!?" I've only read about these kinds of instructions, never have I witness this in my time.

I had always heard about this, but I am seeing it, and still not believing! I was getting pretty hungry, and there was a familiar sign that I knew about in my time, it was a Hamburger & Hot dog Diner!, so let's go eat! I thought. Upon approaching the front door I was met by a group of angry whites, that informed me that I could not enter in, I knew then it was time to make sure the stone was in my hand, because this may get just a little bit uncomfortable for some of us. No one laid a hand on me, just a lot of shouting, "get away from here Nigga" you don't belong here!", but I was not intimidated by their voices, as long as no one laid a hand on me, nothing was going to happen. I continued inside and I was surprised to see other blacks at the counter bar setting and chanting bible verses, so I two set down at the bar. The waitress came up to me and said: "sorry we don't serve coloreds here, can't you read the sign?" I smiled and said, "ma'am I can read, and that's fine with me cause, I don't eat coloreds, so can I please have a Footlong

Chili Cheese Dog with a Root Beer?". Well I guess that didn't help my situation very much, just made things worse, and I guess because I didn't just recite a verse like the others were doing, I was considered a smart mouth and a trouble maker. Now the crowd of whites are standing directly behind me and shouting unfavorable words at me, and someone poured sugar and cream on my

head and then started doing the same on all the other heads of the blacks that were sitting at the bar as well. We all just set there being humiliated. After pouring the sugar then came the cream, and whatever else that they could find. They are having so much fun, and nothing is being done, we did not put up a fight, we just continued to chant bible verses. No police came to our rescue, they just added to our embarrassment, with a lot of onlookers observing this treatment that we are getting, and then someone decides to strike me and then another and another. Then I thought this was enough, and it had gone too far. What could I do? I thought to myself, this was so funny to them, maybe we too should get a good laugh. I reached into my pocket and clutch the stone for full intensity and shouted "**Switch**!. No, we did not do any more harm to them than what they had done to us, instead, they were just put into our positions with the sugar and cream and setting there with everyone watching how humiliating and embarrassing this was.

The laughing was not at us anymore, but them, and guess who was now standing all around them? Nothing but blacks as far as could be held within the restaurant, and outside. Then came to their rescue three black officers to inform them that they were not to be sitting at the counter to eat, and would need to leave, they would have to make their orders from the outside window.

"you know the rules", the officer replied, and the whites replied "who do you think you're talking too, Nigga!, the officers reply was oh so familiar, "who gave you permission to speak?, I'm sorry but you're under arrest for talking back to an officer of the law Boy!" "I've got sugar and cream all over me, this is so unfair for you to treat us this way!," said the whites, And the officer replied, "and since you got sugar and cream all over you, well, Looks like ya'll been served, now let's go! Hope you enjoy your new shoes, "how are they fitting? I hope they are not too tight.

Chapter 7
"I lied, and I am so sorry"

This journey is taking me back in time to a northern part of Arkansas, a town called Gassville which is close to the most prejudice town in Arkansas called Cotter, word has it no blacks could reside there. "why am I here, I asked." The stone was put into a position where once again I would not be seen, and probably best that I am not seen, because chances may not be that great for getting through one night in this place. The Stone and I have travel back into a time of July 20, 1940. I found myself walking with two other black men late on a Saturday night, it seems as though they had been out at their local juke joint and were heading home on a quiet dark road, they were quite comfortable with the walk and just making conversation, when up in the distance they heard noises that they were not sure of so they went cautiously closer and when they got there they notice a white couple making love.

The couple notice the two black men approaching as well, their faces were very familiar. The lady was married to a very upstanding official in the local town and the man she was with was just a low life with not much to write home about, who seem to always be in trouble, and not someone she wanted the town knowing that she'd been seeing. The two men and the couple's faces met "you better not say a word boys at what you just saw!" the men's response was "we didn't see nothing mister, we ain't seen a thang mister! we won't say a word!". The young white lady was not buying the fact that they would not tell, she knew if it got back to her husband it was going to be all over, so she thought her best way out was to scream Rape, Rape, those Nigga Boys Raped me, Help! Help! Of course, her lover caught on real quick to this great idea, which would be his cover-up as well, and they took their new act on the road! And the two men being totally surprised by this new-found act decided that they could not talk their way out of this, it would be best to run, and run they did! As they were making there way home, it was not long before the posses were on their way with a vengeance on their mind. The truck pulled up outside one of the men's house and demanded that the man to come out or they would burn the house down. After the standoff, the door opened and the man came out with his mother and father and other siblings. The men on the truck grab the black man and asked the young white lady that was accusing them "is this the guy?" and her reply was "yes! That's him!" "No!" said the mother of the black man, No!", "Oh God Please!, No!, Ma'am Please have mercy on my Son, he said he didn't do anything to you! why are you doing this to my son?" with a cold look, the young white lady replied to the men, "it was him!". The men proceeded to throw a rope over a tree limb to hang the young black man.

Well, well the Big sheriff has made it on the scene chewing on his two-day-old cigar, and is doing absolutely nothing to stop this event instead he says, "Let's get this thang over with boys, no need to be out here all nite." The rope was around the man's neck, I knew that something needed to be done, but what? An innocent man is being hung just to protect her status! no way! Not tonight! I wanted my focus to be on the young white lady the accuser. The Stone was being held and the intensity was building fast. I spoke the word "**Switch!**". I was not sure what the outcome was going to be, but it was a good change. It was discovered that the young white lady the accuser has a teenage son around the age of 17 or 18 years of age. The hanging is about to take place, and she looks up to witness the hanging and discovers that the black man was no longer the one with the noose around his neck, it was her son now being hung.

"Wait!" she screamed, "Wait!" that's my son! "what are you doing?, how did my son get here!?", as she ran to the men holding the rope, she screamed "what are you doing?", as the men began to pull up on the rope said "this mother has stated that your son Raped her Daughter.
What? What Are you talking about? My son has not done anything, "you need to talk to the mother, she has the last say so," said the men holding the rope. Now the young white lady is begging for the mercy of her son, "Please ma'am" don't have my son hung, please don't hang him! He's so innocent! Confused the young white lady was, and yes she did remember where she was just a few minutes ago with the final word of a death sentence to another mother's innocent son. "I am so sorry for lying on your son Ma'am", the black mother is looking at her completely confused, thinking "what is she talking about?". Please forgive me for lying about your son, I never knew it was this much pain for fearing that my son could be innocently killed.

I never took the time to understand why your pleadings with me to have mercy on your son, and now here I am begging you for the mercy of my Son, "Please have mercy, Please!", as she continued to beg.

The Black mother just looked ahead with a very stern face, and said to the men that were holding the rope, "He's the one, hang him!" No!," the young white lady Screamed, "No!" as the rope was being pulled up, I was holding the Stone and it was already very hot to the touch, and I said, "**Switch**". At the moment the young lady still looking at the hanging taking place and she notices that her son was no longer on the other end of the robe, but it was the young black man that was once again at the end of the rope. She ran toward the men that were pulling on the robe she grabbed them and shouted as loud as she could, "Stop!, Stop!, I lied, this man is innocent! The Man is innocent! Stop! They were amazed at her actions, and they complied with her. The young black man was let down and freed.

The young white lady went up to the mother of the black man crying and repeating I am so sorry, I am so sorry Ma'am! Somehow I was you for just a few moments it was as if I was wearing your shoes. I could feel all your fears and your cry for mercy for your son, I felt it all, and I am so sorry I lied just to protect my status. How could I have been so heartless, and cruel to you? I think from now on every day I know I will be reminded of having worn your shoes. I will forever see the life of others from a different set of eyes. I am so Sorry!

Chapter 8
The fifth Discovery
The Plantation

I always wanted to see for myself the life on the plantation, I knew I'd never make it very long if I had to endure that lifestyle, but something was calling me to be a witness in the unfair madness. I knew the Stone would be my shield but had no idea the extreme madness and inhumane life that I was to be swept into until it all happened, and no more wandering, this was Real!

Again because of the way I held the Stone I was just an onlooker my presence was not known by anyone. I prepared myself for the journey I placed the Stone in my left back pocket, I began to rub it continuously and the thoughts were giving to me "August 16, 1850, the place Jacksonville, Florida location is the Kingsley Plantation. I found myself walking down a lonely road seemingly through a marsh or swampland, the road was called Palmetto Road. I could see in a distant something coming my way, as I got closer there were people walking and were in chains. Their clothes were barely on, and they had no shoes, these were slaves! They were looking very worn. I stopped as they passed by and stared with disbelief, there was a man on a horse with a whip and was popping it at the slaves as they slowly walked by my presence, I guess maybe they were off on a work detail. I did not interfere, I continued walking to the plantation where I had been driven mentally to do. I could see in a distance large trees and fields of vegetation all around, the house was very large, there were small hut-like houses all around. As I came upon the property I could hear singing off in a distant field, Man! I thought, Listen to that harmony! As I came upon the property, I could see the true signs of slavery there was so much sadness that I could see towards these slaves. The living conditions were horrible, the houses don't have floors just the bare ground, a large rag hung over the doors.

Outside There was a man strung up to a tree and getting beaten bareback, and why? I wondered.

There were onlookers and nothing that they could do or say, just look sadly at their friend or love one as the whip continue to come down. I wanted to make a difference, but something was silently saying not at this time. I continued observing the surroundings of power over the slaves. I came in view of the master of the plantation Master Kingsley in the flesh, a mean selfish, heartless man with no sympathy towards any of his slaves. I saw him do harm to a slave child, he grabbed him up by his loose fitting shirt and slap him hard because he found him reading with his white son, "little Nigga, you can't read, and you better not let me catch you reading ever again, or I will whip you, your momma, and your daddy!. It was so belittling and controlling of what the slaves have to go thru. Again, the suggestion was given to me not now can the Stone be used. I continued walking through the yard and Oh! it was a hot August summer day, and I wondered about the breaks that the field workers should be getting, but they were made to toil on until the sun was about to give up the day. I found myself inside the Big house.

I saw a very fine complexed young lady, she was dressed differently from the other slaves, and not much work did I see her doing, I don't think she's the master's wife, but there's something different about her. Oh! Now I understand, she's Master Kingsley's Lover, and Master Kingsley's wife or the slave girl's parents have no say so in this matter.

I could smell the aroma coming from somewhere around back, it seems they have to cook outside in a smaller cabin in order to keep the big house from getting too hot in the summer. It was time to eat, and all the Kingsley family members had gathered to eat, but the slaves who had cooked the food are not allowed in to enjoy the eating of this fine meal, but instead, they have to take the scraps of what might be left over, which is never very much. As the night began to move on toward the midnight hour, and silence began to become the time for total rest. I thought that now would be a good time for the slaves to leave this place, but no one was packing up leaving. The voice of suggestions was given that now was the time to use the power of the Stone. As I approached the main house, I had my hand on the Stone in my left back pocket I could feel it getting warmer and warmer, it was going to have to be as warm as I could stand it, because I was going to need all the power that it possessed to accomplish this next task. I stepped into the house, I walked into all the rooms that were being occupied by the master's family. I laid eyes on each of them. It was necessary that I saw them all, my eyes needed to see them. After seeing everyone in the main house I went to the quarters where all the slave drivers were resting and laid eyes on them. When all had been seen I then walked through the slave quarters and laid eyes on them as well.

When I had made all the rounds necessary, I walked out to the front of the plantation and oh the Stone was beyond warm, it was Hot! Hot! And then I knew the time was now. I shouted in a very loud voice, "**SWITCH!, SWITCH!!**

As the early morning came, and their eyes started to come open to a new day all that was seen through my eyes were going to have a new day. So wake up! And see this new day!

Chapter 9
A Reversal was Made

Morning came with a great surprise. There is something strange taking place as they all began to wake up. This reminds me of the time when I stopped by the Planet of the Apes, (oh! Boy! What a **Switch** that was). Now on the Plantation The whites were still white, and the blacks were still black, but the blacks were no longer slaves, they were wise, educated and very much in charge, and they knew it! And yes, they carried the hatred and controlling attitude that the Kingsley master had, exactly the same, (No compassion or mercy) Master Kingsley is now being woke up by his new-found master, which he has no idea what has just happened to him, was he dreaming?

A scream rings out "get out of that bed, and let's go to work", and the whip cracks across his body, and Boy! Was he surprised, Master Kingsley who is now a slave who tries to speak boldly to who he thought was still his slave, but to no avail, and upon going outside he discovered that everything was different all the blacks were dress to the finest, and all the whites had been given the gift of total slavery with all the trimmings. They even had a new dress code, rags for clothes, and no shoes. They were considered dumb and uneducated, they were beaten for their lack of work. The hours were long and hard, and each time master Kingsley tried to speak he was beaten for talking back to his new master and was strung up to a tree and given his lashes. The food that was given was not fit for the dogs, but that's what he and his family had to eat. How could anyone be treated so badly, Master Kingsley thought, "why are they treating me so bad, and talking down to me, I know I am better than this how can anyone be so cruel". I rubbed the Stone in my Right hand and return to the present day for a while. It was best that I leave things as they were and return at a later time, I felt it was necessary that time was needed for master Kingsley's family and friends to really get a full understanding of how one should be treated, and what it feels like to have to go through life in a continuous time of daily suffering and unimaginable abuse. And yes, for History sake I did return back and the **switch** was made, and the overall attitude at Kingsley Plantation was never the same.

Chapter 10
The Stone necklace
The Six Discovery
No Power

Something was driving me to make a necklace so that the stone could be worn around my neck. There had to be a reason for this, but I had no idea why. I tried moving back and forth in time by rubbing with my left and right hands, and it all seems to be working as before when it was in my pocket. The power to touch and **Switch** was still true. I was being summoned to the 7th day of April in the year 33 A.D., Why, I wondered. I've entered into a very strange land, I can not recognize my surroundings, my attire is all too different I have no pants!, Where, are my pants? I'm wearing a robe! where are my pockets? I had my Right hand on the Stone which was around my neck, just in case I needed to return to the present day in a quick hurry. I was surrounded by a multitude of people, they all seem to be in a rush and going the same way.

"what's going on?" I wondered. I could hear shouting and cheering. It seems I am in a medieval time; do I see Roman soldiers? Where am I?

The crowd has stopped and have gathered, it seems like they are all watching a parade or something. I push myself through to the front of the crowd, I look both ways up and down the path, but I see nothing coming or going. What are they looking for? I wondered. I could see Roman soldiers coming and pushing everyone back, something is coming, I could hear shouting, crying and booing. There was an unusual sound that I could hear in a distance, it sounded like something dragging, I could hear a whipping sound. Around the corner slowly moving was the image of a man dragging a cross! Oh! My LORD! This can't be! It's JESUS! On his way to Calvary to die on the Cross! Oh my LORD!

He was getting closer and closer, oh! And the pain I could see it all over his face, and what pain did I see! He's so close to coming by me, coming directly in front of me!

"What could I do?" I thought to my self, "what could I do? I could feel his pain, I wondered if maybe through the Stone I could bear some of his pain if maybe I could ease the suffering that he was going through. Oh! How I felt his pain! I held the Stone in my right hand and held on for the warmth of power it would produce, and as he passed by close enough that I could reach out and touch him, He fell to the ground with his cross, and I thought, "here's my chance to make a difference". I reached down to help JESUS up and in doing so I placed my arm under his shoulder to pull him up, and by me now touching him the **Switch** should have been made, and I should begin to feel all his pain and suffering, but I felt nothing!

I felt nothing! Now I was puzzled with the power of the Stone, nothing happened! There was no **Switch**! JESUS looked me straight in the eyes as the blood was streaming down his face, he shook his head and said softly "this is not meant for you", and with all the strength he had left within his frail body, JESUS slowly marched on, carrying his cross on up Calvary's Hill. I continued to march at a distant behind Jesus to a place called Golgotha "place of the skull". They hung him between to thieves as I listened closely I heard Jesus Ask his father to forgive them for they know not what they do. Later there was a conversation among the two thieves one railed on Jesus saying "If thou be Christ save thyself and us", but yet the other thief answered rebuking him saying "Thus not thou fear God? Seeing that thou are in the same condemnation, and we indeed justly for we received the due reward of our deeds, but this man has done nothing amiss, and he said to Jesus "Lord remember me when thou cometh into thy kingdom". And I heard Jesus answer him saying "verily, verily I say unto thee, today shalt thou be with me in **Paradise**". Wow! I just witness a most powerful **Switch**! There was an instant **Switch** from Sin to Salvation, a Reversal was made for this Thief on the cross to a brand new destination, **Paradise.**

Between the sixth and the ninth hour there was total darkness and earth shaking disturbances. Jesus Spoke in a very loud voice "Father into thou hands I commend my spirit" and he gave up the ghost. I could hear others saying "truly this was a righteous man."

As I wondered back at my trying to make a difference in the pain and suffering of Jesus I stood there stunned at what had happened, the Stone had always worked, but this time when I thought it was well worth the **Switch** it had failed, it had no effect, it had no power, "Why", I asked myself, "Why?

Chapter 11
The Seventh Discovery
The Voice

Suddenly everything became silent, no noise from the crowd, not a sound from the soldier's whip or their marching feet, just complete silence and total stillness. Then there was that bright light that I saw the night all this started, the light was blinding! And Oh So Warm! And so soothing, then a voice spoke to me! A voice clear, and so real, it spoke to me! "Fear Not, don't be alarmed, Oh my Servant of Time Travels, your reasons for being here were all mine, all of your travels back in time was suggested by me. I sent the Stone to you. I was testing your passion, and your heart,

I was testing your sincere desire to make a difference in the suffering of others." "Your mission was to witness total suffering beyond the measure of mankind, and you did, and this was a true test of how you would want to bear the cross for my Son JESUS, although you did try and show me that you have a strong compassion for mankind,

and that you would even take up the cross, and you did well, but Oh My Servant of Time Travels, this was not your cross to bear, only my Son JESUS can take up the sins of this world, he and only he can bear the cross, and die for the world's suffering, and his power is far beyond the Stone, for he is the Rock, he has All Power in the Heavens and the Earth. You have proved yourself well, and my Blessing will be upon you. Go back to your time and share your story to others of how important it is to have the love and passion, the consideration and understanding of one's suffering, and what can be done to ease their suffering, and pain. Tell them that today may be their day to be up and well, but tomorrow is not promise that it will be the same

*Tell them to make a mental **Switch** and see how it feels to be in the one's shoes that are suffering, and to make a difference. And be not the one that is responsible for their suffering, don't be the cause. And if I see that they will not, then I, the Great **I AM**, will take it upon myself to make the **Switch**, I will Make **the REVERSAL**.*

Chapter 12
"Just a Rock"
"and Somebody Told Me"

*F*or the last time I held the stone in my right hand and begin to rub, and the warmth continued to increase as I started my travel back to my home and time. Today is Saturday, July 1, 2000. It seemed as though I'd been gone forever but only a few days. My journey was now complete. The travels are all but gone now, and the stone had served its usefulness. The brightness has started to dim and the radiance and sparkle had all but gone. The multi-colors have settled to just one. Now in my hand, all I hold is just a Rock.
"Wake up, Wake up", There's that voice again speaking to me, *"Wake up, and deliver this message, wake up and tell your story to others."* What?

"You Mean to tell me I was dreaming?" I've never been within a dream that was so real, so vivid and revealing. What a journey that was! I just knew that I had been in all those places! This was so real to me! So it was not the power that is within the Stone, but the Power that we already have, it's the power that is within our hearts and minds to make the **Switch**.

He woke me up this morning and told me to deliver this message, and HE said you'll be sure and know who HE is. Hmm! Somebody told me to deliver this message, and pass it on to you, HE said the time has come for us to have a change in our hearts and minds.

"Wake up and deliver this message, and pass this on."
"Have a Reversal of the Mind and Heart"

"This is not the End, but the Beginning of a Mind Change within you"

"lasreveR ehT"

Verses To Consider

MATTHEW 7:12
Therefore all things whatsoever ye would that men should do to you, do ye even so to them: for this is the law and the Prophets.   Kjv.

Luke 6:31
And as ye would that men should do to you, do ye also to them likewise.   Kjv.

Romans 15:1-2
We who are strong have an obligation to bear with the failing of the weak, and not to please ourselves.
Let each of us please his neighbor for his good, to build them up.   Niv.

Made in the USA
Coppell, TX
20 January 2026

68497417R10042